A Gronking to Remember

Book One in the Rob Gronkowski Erotica Series

LACEY NOONAN

CONTENTS

ACKNOWLEDGMENTS

I would like to thank Leigh, Dan, Chad, Greg, Craig, Steve, Craig, Greg, Another Chad?, Mike, Stephen, the people at the library, the neighbors, the security and police and crowd at Gillette Stadium and most of all, the Big Man himself, Gronkalish, for making this fantasy come true.

I

I'll never forget the first time I saw Gronk spike a football. It changed my life forever.

The unrivaled power of his touchdown dance: "The Gronk." It jettisoned jiggling ribbons of electric jelly through my body and melted my knees like two pads of margarine—turned me on quicker and made me wetter than at any other time in my life besides my wedding night.

"Who…" I said, walking all the way into the den from the kitchen—getting a drink after an intense sewing session that had left my hands pleasantly sore—and stood behind the couch. "Who…"

"What?" my husband, Dan, asked with a peevish tone to his voice. Wifey no speaky during

Man Smashy Time.

"Who… who's that?" I said, "The guy who just *did* that. That football throw down thing."

"Come on, Leigh! That's Gronk!" one of Dan's friends shouted from across the room.

I laughed.

Gronk? It was such a weird word. Like something a caveman would say. But the name made sense with what I saw on the gigantic flatscreen TV over the fireplace. "What's a 'Gronk?'" I asked.

"Gron*kowski*. Rob Gronkowski," Dan said.

"Hmm…" I said, sticking my finger absentmindedly between my teeth and swiveling my torso slowly at the hips.

I should start off by saying that I'm not one of those women who like football. I mean, you see them—the women in the jerseys and whatnot—in the stands at games, acting all frenzied and squeezed all around by burly, hairy, ape-like, oily, wild-eyed, vicarious-glory-engorging, howling-insane men and you have to wonder: do they really understand what's going on out there on the field? Are they just there to keep an eye on their husbands, make sure they don't fall over a balcony? Or are the enticements of overpriced, bland hot dogs and Bud Lite really too much to turn down for these ladies of the "Gridiron Appreciation Club?"

On the screen they showed a slow motion replay of the Gronk-man catching a football and then barreling his way through three other smaller men onto a colored part of the field I later learned was called the "end zone." His body was large, and even though he had on lots of pads under his outfit and a big round helmet, you could tell how muscled he was, how fit and bulging he was everywhere.

It's hard to explain exactly, but seeing such a fierce display of physical domination on the TV made me feel like a *woman*.

I felt instantly small and tender and moist. I felt susceptible and presentable. My body and soul were the complete opposite of what was happening in the game and I felt a sort of warm glow pulsating inside my stomach.

As far as Sundays in November went it was a typical Sunday in November in our household. My husband had a few of his shapeless friends over for a football game. And there they all were, two or three guys named Steve, a Todd, a Mike, there might have been a Greg or a Craig, possible a Tad or Chad? spread around the room, a small cluster of them at the coffee table, which was covered in chips and dips and half empty beer bottles. It was guts, farts and sports gear aplenty.

It wasn't my scene, to say the least, but I came into the den and sat down next to Dan. My sewing could wait, I thought—could go to hell for all I cared. Suddenly all I wanted to do was watch Gronk do his thang-thang in the zone place there. My vagina demanded it.

"So, like, what teams are playing?" I asked, squinting at the abbreviations next to the score. "STL and NE… Seattle and who else? NE? Nebraska?"

A couple of guys laughed. There was crunching and slurping and the metallic yawn of a reclining chair going back.

"Jesus, Leigh," Dan said.

"What? Who's playing is all I want to know."

Dan laughed into his upturned bottle of Molson Extra Gold. "Since when do you care about football?" he asked, still peeved.

"I am interested in all of humanity," I said, "And as inhumane as these pituitary monsters are behaving to one another, I am willing to bare witness for the greater sake of humanity."

This soliloquy/weirdness had the wanted effect of at least shutting Dan up, since some of the guys laughed. If I had pierced the invisible wall of his special Sunday Boy's Club, there was nothing he could say about it now. Dan and I had been going through some difficulties for a while. And after six years together, I knew that I would be hearing about it later when the guys left—but I would cross that bridge when I came to it, I thought.

I nestled in on the couch, curled my legs up under me. Maybe I would get to see Gronk spike another football through my heart. The game continued.

And the game continued.

And continued.

Continuing some more, the game then proceeded to continue continuing after that.

All that green field and mindless colorful malaise of padded bodies. Nothing made sense. And my thoughts began to wander again across the kitchen to my sewing studio, my darning needles, my waiting *Leclerc Voyageur* table loom, my purl ones, my knit twos.

Then suddenly there was a commotion in the room. I refocused my eyes on the TV.

"Brady in the shotgun…" the TV announcer said… "steps back in the pocket… Shane Vereen in the backfield… play action… a Gronkowski fade route… Brady unloads… Gronk catches… breaks a tackle… makes for the middle… breaks another… LOOK at that block… Knocking on the door of the house… fifteen… ten… five… touchdown Gronkowski!"

My heart leaped in my chest. It was thudding. There were groans and cheers throughout the room.

I stood.

On the TV I watched the incredibly large man spazz out with joy. He was surrounded by his teammates, mere munchkins by comparison. They surrounded him, like little supplicants around a holy mountain, but he scattered them away.

"Oh, here it comes," the announcer said.

"Oh yes," said another voice.

"The Gronk. Look out everyone!"

Gronk lifts the football in his hand and spikes it down with such violence the ball launches fifty feet in the air and into the crowd of the stadium, who flip out wrestling to get the holy token of pigskin.

Needless to say, I am weakened again by the spectacle. Silky ribbons of juicy pleasure wobble through my nethers. My nipples harden beneath my sweater. I am hot. The room around me recedes. My breath quickens. I squeeze my hands together in the center of my chest, between my breasts.

I'm about to pass out when a needly nasal voice startles me from my reverie.

"What the hell is wrong with you, Leigh?"

It is my husband, Dan. Daniel, my husband of six years.

"I…" I manage to stammer out. "Nothing," I say.

Should I say anything about what I'm feeling? About how I am so insanely turned on by watching a hulking man ten years younger than me—a mere boy—spiking a football on TV? It's so absurd—it was new to me. I couldn't imagine what the fellas in the room would have said. They would have laughed and then I'd have to hear about it from their idiot wives later at some get together.

But lucky for me Dan isn't that perceptive.

"Since you're leaving can you bring in those three extra six packs from the garage before you disappear into *Yarnia*?"

I take a few breaths. They're playing the touchdown and monster spiking again on the TV in slow motion and I can feel my pussy wetting in my panties, but I maintain my composure. I straighten myself out. Six pack? I bet Gronk has a six pack you could wash laundry on. I lick my lips thinking about it.

"S-sure," I say and walk out to the garage.

It's November and we live in Connecticut. The garage is cold. My nipples, already hard, erect further into the soft wool of my white sweater, a comfy cozy little number I darned up a couple years ago during a Corriedale phase.

I reach for the refrigerator door where Dan keeps his extra football beer but my hand doesn't make it…

Nope, not at all…

My fingers take a detour to the front my pants. I back up against the door to the kitchen and sink my hand all the way down the front of my panties into my hot pussy and begin furiously rubbing my clit.

"Oh… ooh…" I moan to myself.

I picture being mauled by a huge monolith of a man. My body used for his hard pleasure; a stone god gripping me in his hands. He hoists me in the air. My clothes are ripped from my body, my quivering flesh open and available, my body ready to be used by the strong force of the universe, a ravaging, rampaging man. He brushes aside his loincloth. And then... out comes his stone pillar of a cock.

And then he takes me...

Within seconds I come. My back slams against the garage door. I shout out once, twice—stifle myself. "Oh, God," I moan, my voice loose and hoarse, then: "Wow!"

The orgasm is primordial, primeval, intense, insane.

I compose myself and go back into the house and go into the kitchen. In a mirror by the back stairs I look at myself. My round cheeks are flushed, my light brown hair is mussed. Is that a tear on my cheek, just below my soft blue eye? And then a little cool breeze on my skin informs me of something—I look down and realize my jeans are still undone. Smiling, I zip them up.

I drift into the den. The game is still on. The men are staring intently at it, as if trying to divine magic secrets, like wizards around a crystal ball or something, trying, it seems to me, to figure out how one might squeeze blood from a stone.

I plop down next to Dan.

"Ummm… what the shit, Leigh? You seriously forgot the beer? What were you doing in the garage?" he says peevishly, so peevishly in fact, that it feels like he's jabbed a sewing needle into my ear.

II

Next Sunday couldn't come fast enough. The week trudged by. At strange times I would catch myself thinking about *that spike*.

Ah, that spike…

The image of the performance would creep into my head during conversations at work at the library and I'd have to mentally buckle down and keep myself from saying out loud: "*But Dat Spike Doe.*" Where this was all coming from on a deeper level I couldn't say, but I certainly knew what was responsible, or who. The Gronk.

So that was my frame of mind when all of Dan's friends one-by-one materialized at our door and were ushered again into our den for another Sunday full of televised American NFL

Football.

I tried to play it cool. I stayed upstairs and didn't come down right away, pacing back and forth for a few minutes, wanting to come down so bad—so, so very bad—and watch the game. To see what illicit pleasures it had in store for me.

Finally I couldn't take it any more. *What if I miss it!?* I yelled to myself in my head, fear bubbling up in my heart.

Quickly, I scampered down the stairs in my socks and made for the kitchen. The sounds of the game, the white-noise-roar of the crowd punctuated by the little titters of the referee whistles, filled the whole downstairs.

Same as last week, all the men were planted throughout the den. I hung out by the door watching the TV. Five, ten, fifteen minutes went by and there was no mention of Gronk or Gronkowski or anything that would make my panties wet. They were bone dry and I was getting annoyed. I grew impatient.

What bullshit was this?

I sauntered into the den and sat next to Dan on the couch during a commercial, a Cialis ad starring what looked like a decrepit CEO and young prostitute driving around Napa Valley in a convertible.

All the men seemed to have assigned seats in the den. Dan was in the middle of the couch with one of the Gregs or Craigs on his right, but no one on his left, same as before.

I let a few pregnant seconds pass.

"Where's Gronk?" I finally asked.

No one responded. A beer was opened. A tortilla chip lifted three quarters of a cup of pine-apple-chipotle salsa to a quivering mouth.

I exhaled through my nose, made some faces, trying to stitch together the courage to ask the room full of men again just what in the Sam Hill was going on here.

"Um… where's Gronk—Rob Gronkowski?" I asked again. "Is he playing today?"

"What? He's on the Patriots. That's a different game, Leigh," Dan said.

"Well, can we watch that game instead?"

The air seemed to leave the whole room. The temperature dropped twenty degrees and I could feel Dan turning his head towards me very slowly and dramatically as if it were on some kind of pulley system in a horror circus. I pretended not to see it, but I could feel his eyes burning on my cheek.

Then, perhaps ennobled by the sexualized warrior spirit of the Gronk, I turned to face Dan. He had a small, round face, dark hair and brown eyes. Horror circus—did he really look like a marionette puppet? The ol' weekend grizzle was on his chin. And there was a sarcastic and questioning smile on his thin lips.

"*What?*" I ventured.

"What do you mean *what?* I'm the one who's saying *what?*"

"Heck, you know I'm a Pats fan," one of the other guys interrupted. "I don't mind if we switch."

"Chad, this is a Jets house and you know it," Dan said, suddenly turning to the room. "You wanna watch the Patsies play you can go down to McBeery's 'n watch the game with all the other old boozers."

This Chad fellow made a face and by way of reply shuffled some chips around in a bowl.

Something occurred to me. "Wait. Patriots," I said. "The New England Patriots. Right? We're in New England, Dan. Aren't we? This is Connecticut."

"So?"

"Aren't they your team?"

15

"No."

"So you're like a traitor or something. To your people."

There were some laughs in the room. And an accidental fart, probably jarred loose from the uncommon commotion.

"I don't even know *where* to start with *that*," replied Dan.

"Leigh's got a point," Chad—my sweet Chad—said.

"This is a Jets house and this has always been a Jets house!" Dan shouted, angry. Why the hell was he so angry?

I learned out later of course that though nearly all of New England were fans of Boston teams there was a smidge of Connecticut down near New York City that rooted for New York teams. (A dirty little smidge, like the chocolate brown star on the body of an otherwise milky smooth goddess.) Whether you want to consider them traitors is up to you (they are), but at the time this was all news to me and anyway besides the point. The reason I was even in that room that day was for altogether *other* reasons—sexed-up horny, spurned housewife reasons.

"What are the Jets this year so far?" Chad

went on. "Two and Seven?"

"Grrr…" Dan said.

"You might wanna start thinking about switching teams, Dan, is all," Chad continued. "I mean Rex is a helluva coach, I guess, if you like your team to get real up close and personal to kissing Belichik's rings and all."

Dan stood and full-on shrieked at the room: "MOTHERFUCKER get the *fuck* outta this house you wanna keep that up!!!"

"Jesus," someone other than Chad, so I'm guessing a Jets fan (as Chad seemed to be the only one defending the Patriots and my line of inquiry) gruffed into the now-acrid atmosphere of the room.

Dan plomped back down on the couch next to me and stared at the TV. He lifted a bottle of beer to his lips and drank heavily. The liquid drained into his throat and he slammed the bottle down on the glass coffee table. He picked up another one and opened it.

The game resumed. Food was scarfed. Drinks drunk. People forgot about the conversation.

But not me.

I sat there as long as I could stomach it. I

wanted to reach over and scratch Dan's eyes out with my fingernails. Why was he being such a fucking asshole? *Grrr…* I growled to myself in my questioning, unsatisfied noggin. I looked at Dan and saw all of his faults magnified times a thousand. I couldn't even think of the last time we'd had full-on romantic sex. We had sex of course, once a week at the most. We didn't have kids yet, so it was easy to do. *God, did I even want to have kids with this guy?* I found myself thinking. And then I was horrified at that thought. Not because of the content of it, but because now I was questioning the totality of our relationship.

I got up quickly from the couch and went to wander around the house. I was annoyed. I was titillated. I was scared. I was bold. I was nervous. I was optimistic. I didn't know what I wanted. I was a woman.

Then I knew what I wanted…

Upstairs, soft socks padding on thick rug, I crept into Dan's office. I sneaked behind his desk and fired up his computer.

Moving quickly, I went to YouTube and searched "Gronk spike." For my efforts I was rewarded with a full assortment of videos. Fingers trembling on the mouse, I clicked one…

The video window is small so I move in real close. It's the typical side view of a bunch of players. There is the announcer's voice again. "Play action… two wide-outs, Gronk to the right of the line…"

My heart skips a beat at mention of the name. I search him out. Which one is he? Before I can find him though, the play starts. The colors on the field swirl like ingredients in a mixing bowl.

The quarterback drops back and throws the football.

A giant male ox catches the ball, tucks it under his huge biceps and turns upfield. A smattering of wee players in black costumes form a little pile of hors d'oeuvres between him and the end zone. They are no match for him of course. Because it's Gronk.

Rob Gronkowski lowers his shoulder and batters through the defenders like a bowling ball and they fly away into the gutters of history. Gronk stomps into the end zone and leaps in the air. Victory! Victory is his!

I hold my breath. This is it. My left hand slides up the inside of my thigh. Here it comes…

Gronk raises the football high above him.

And then he swings it down with utmost velocity. The ball impacts on the ground, and I feel it in my body—that's how *into it* I am—and the ball shoots sideways at a referee. The referee barely gets out the way. He looks like a scared little goose with terrible reflexes as the brown football whizzes past his frightened face.

Gronk's teammates once again surround him. They hug. They high-five. They jump up in the air into each other's backs.

Fuck yes.

I unzip the front of my pants and slide two fingers down my front. I was so focused on the play that I hadn't realized how wet I'd gotten. My panties were dripping wet!

Quickly I slide my fingers down into my pussy, curling them and sinking them upward inside myself.

I imagine myself in football equipment. It's late at night in the locker room. Everyone's gone. The lights are low. But there I am, looking sweet in my gear. A pretty pink uniform. But pantsless, my bare ass on the cool wooden bench. I am lost in thought. I am a princess in this place and then I hear it with my princess ears. On the other side of the locker room someone is taking a shower.

Annoyed that my castle should be used this late at night, that my domain be invaded by some *prole*, I walk towards the noise. At the end of a row of lockers I turn a corner and there he is. It's a giant of a man. A warrior. A knight. His muscles ripple in the soft light and splash of water coming from the shower head. His buttocks are sublime. Men shouldn't be this shapely, I think to myself in the fantasy, but my eyes are not deceiving me, as I drop one foot daintily, then the other onto the tile floor of the steaming shower. He is that gorgeous.

In Dan's office, I flick my fingers up and down over my clitoris with one hand and stroke the fingers of the other into my pussy. Waves of pleasure beset my being. The passion surges in my body—my body: hot. My head is growing weak. My legs are trembling below the desk. Losing it, losing it, my body grows limp and swivels the ergonomic chair. I spread my legs as far as they will go in my tight jeans.

"Fuck!" I shout. I don't care if anyone hears me. "Oh yes!"

My eyes flutter. Deep reds and pulsating purples blind my vision. I've never felt such pleasure. The colors wobble: I wobble too. It flips me in and out, in and out, and then…

They show the spike in slow motion and POW!

The chair beneath me rattles. My brain grows dizzy. Everything in the room is light.

I come.

So hard.

I actually slide off the chair onto the floor, where my orgasm continues. It swells and swells. It keeps going, turning me into a thudding mess. Fuck. Football! Oh, God. My bare ass is on the floor now, my pants around my ankles as the climax washes over my body like a powerful storm, washing over me like the most powerful Tight End the NFL has ever seen washing over a weak secondary.

My bare butt bounces up and down, my hands stroking and pinching and teasing myself, my juices running over the floor.

"Spike me! Spike me!" I shout.

Then, my orgasm subsides on sweet little waves of dwindling pleasure.

I try to catch my breath. The room is hot, spinning, like a ride at an amusement park in the humid heat of summer.

And then—as if grinding the whole gronking, spinning rainbow ride of humid joy to a halt—Dan walks right into the goddamn office.

III

From there on out, I was sold on the powers of Gronk.

Whenever I could get a chance at work all that next week I would sneak away to a dark corner of the library and fire up a computer. I'd google info on Gronkowski, check his stats, read his bio, watch some videos, then rub one out right then and there in the library—let jiggly ribbons of lady-sensuality cavort on my body, strangle me, swallow me whole and annihilate me in its pink and roiling rivers and flowers and mountains... Until I'd hear voices approaching in the stacks and quickly zip up and abscond away with my nasty and naughty secrets.

It was dangerous. I knew that. If I ever got

caught tickling the pink at work there would be serious consequences. Even criminal. I was playing with fire.

But what could I do? My whole being was on fire. This new chapter—this Chapter Called *Gronk*—had touched a spark to my soul which had lain so dormant for so long.

I was aching for a love pummeling. Dan and I had been on the outs. And that hurts. When a relationship ends, the pain grows exponentially. In addition to the simple pain of love's acidic dwindling, both members will fight it before they admit what is happening. They let denial in, they argue. Better to just let it all fall away... But this is so easy to say—and a million times harder to do. At the time, I was in the thick of it.

But back to Dan's office...

Lucky for me I have a quick mind. I can come up with a good lie in a heartbeat. I took an improv class when I was in college.

Plus, Dan was plastered.

When Dan blundered into his office I was ass-butt-naked on the floor behind his desk, my pussy still throbbing from the wild and natural orgasm. He wobbled in, said, "Wha tha fa, Leigh? Wha tha fa you doin' down dere?" and listed against the doorjamb. He was angry too. I could tell by his tone of voice the Jets had lost.

Moving like a jackrabbit I zipped up my pants and pretended to be looking for a pen. "Gol dangit," I said, and, "Where's that dang pen?" getting up from behind the desk. Dan had wobbled over in the meantime. I had forgotten to close the window. The Gronk video was still there. "Wha the fa's this, Leigh? Wha the faaaaaa you watchin' Patsy games for ya *beyotch*?"

"I—"

But before I could respond he'd gone through to the bathroom to throw up. Taking this as my chance, I closed the browser window and escaped the office, went straight into the master bath and jumped in the shower, washing away any juicy evidence of my shenanigans and crawled into bed. By the time Dan crawled in next to me, I was pretending to snore.

The next morning I made obtuse references to the office scene, but Dan in his drunkenness had forgotten all about it.

I breathed easy. My secret was safe.

And then before I knew it… It was Sunday again!

Game day.

Hell yes.

This was going to be a doozy. I had done tons of research—or rather, research had been inserted into me by accident as a byproduct of surfing the web for Gronkalicious pussy-stroking material. There was no reason for me to go skulking around upstairs that day because it was a Divisional game: NE at NYJ. New England Patriots at the New York Jets. Both Chad and Dan would have their pineapple-chipotle salsa and eat it too.

Then, like the lame ghosts of lackadaisical loafers too lazy to shuffle off to the next world, the men came, coaxing their tired spirits spiritlessly across the spirit bog to our doorstep: The Gregs, The Craigs, The Mikes, The Steves, The Todds, The Chads. The doorbell rang. In they came, and took root throughout the den once again. Dip jars were unlocked, the trapped air in bags of chips was freed, the skulls of beer bottles were given Indian rugburns till their liquids frothed and debouched. My pussy was wet all day, begging to be fingered.

Fucking fuck I was turned on. Turned on and tuned up since 6 AM when I sat up bolt upright in bed next to a snoozing Husband Dan, stretching my eight fingers and two thumbs for

27

some serious hitchhiking up and down the Gron-kachusetts Turnpike.

Dan was a sour bitch all day. The Jets had been doing terribly all season and this was going to be a bloodbath. New England was riding a six game winning streak. The problem for Dan was that the game was in New York and all fans think they have a better shot of winning at home. Somewhere deep down in Dan's muscle tissue he knew that it was no good though. The Patriots were going to steamroll his team and the different layers of "knowing" were causing misalignments and unpleasant arrangements of the inside of his body and stabbed into the side-gut of his soul—his soul full of bitchy, sour guts.

It was a 1PM game. The game started…

Immediately Gronk lights up the field. He's doing all sorts of cross patterns and Brady is hitting him and Edelman for a TON of dink and dunk yardage since Rex is known as a defensive guru and what that means is that you blitz, so the Jets blitz four out of every five plays and it's backfiring because Brady is reading it and the Patriots are slicing them apart.

"There goes Gronk up the middle," the announcer caws. "Look at that catch! Splits the seam for another fifteen yards, ten of it after the catch."

"I wish he'd split my seam," I mutter to myself. It's near the end of the first quarter.

"Um, what?"

Shit! Dan heard me, I think to myself. I turn, gritting me teeth. No, it's not Dan. It's Chad. At least I think it's Chad. He's standing behind the couch, right behind me. I smile.

"Nothing," I reply to this man I'm possibly at least 50% sure is named Chad.

"Oh, I think I heard *something*," Possible-Chad says and smiles back and runs his hand along the top of the couch. But before things can get icky, Dan turns around to look at him.

"Leave my wife alone, C.H.U.D." he yells. "And get back to your assigned seat by the window. You're fucking up my mojo, Patriots fan."

"I'm pretty sure you could be sitting there with the bloody blessings of eighteen witch doctors and a letter from the Pope and your mojo wouldn't be enough to beat us," Now-I-Know-It's-Chad replies.

"Motherfucker!" Dan yells and begins to stand, trying to look tough, though he's not really that built and only 5'10". Just a regular guy and not a superman of the gridiron like my sweet Gronkalish.

"Okay, okay… Jeez," The Chad-person says and skiffles off back to his seat.

I frown at Dan. "You know, you're being a real kinda—"

"And why the hell are you even here, Leigh? Goddamit! This is really starting to be awful for me," Dan yells, motioning towards the television, then sweeping his arm towards the room, then clenching his fists.

I've never seen this side of him. And it's not a good one. As time has gone on with us, most of Dan's sides have started looking a little unpleasant, and the emergence of this new ugly side has him in danger of sinking below the level of something that is salvageable between us.

"Oh, I'm sorry if I just like spending time with my husband," I say, not without a twist of bitterness, like a lemon rind on a cocktail.

At halftime I bring out a large heavy patchwork quilt I'd made and curl myself into it there on the couch. I feel safe inside it, like a kid in his own world. Dan's bitchiness can't get to me in my world.

But the problem is is that I'm not a kid, and

currently my world involves intense and soaking wet masturbation sessions while watching Robbie G blow apart footballs in end zones.

The second half gets underway and I realize the quilt was a bad idea. Because I'm naughty now; that's the problem. On the screen the Patriots receive the ball for the second half. Instantly, Brady the quarterback starts targeting Gronk. At least twice a set of downs, Gronk's hands are on the ball.

Gronk's hands are on the ball and my hands are on my throbbing pussy. *There's just nowhere else to put them*, I tell myself. *Sorry.*

I begin to masturbate secretly right there in the den surrounded by my husband and his friends. What can I say? The sight of Gronk knocking over little defenders like toy soldiers sends erotic thrills up and down my spine. It turns me the hell on, what's going on in the gladiator ring. Who am I do ignore such dictates from the gods?

It begins with tiny little circles. With the tips of my forefinger and middle finger I rub the pad of skin overtop my pussy. First one way, then the other, clockwise, then the other way. A glow forms in my midsection. My eyes droop, drowsy with pleasure.

"Mmm…" I release from my lips—curled a little now—but quietly. Dan is right next to me and the sound doesn't register with him. I look over and see him staring maniacally at the TV, on the verge of crying. I realize that what Gronk is doing to me is doing the express opposite to Dan.

Poor guy. But so what. None of what is happening on the TV has any real bearing on our lives. Whatever reactions we choose to have we have because we let them.

And boy was I letting it happen!

I spread my legs apart under the blanket. I was hot, really going at my pussy now, fingerbanging myself in front of all these men with both my hands. If only they knew.

"Ooh," I let out.

Dan hears this one.

"What?" he says to me.

I cough, clear my throat. *Good Lord, I almost came*, I tell myself.

"Nothing, I… what was that? What play was that?"

"Only Gronkowski running train on these shitty Jets!" Chad yells from by the window.

"Shut uuuuuuuuuppppp…" Dan laments

back at him, drunker than I thought he was.

"Come ahhhhhhhhhhhhhhhhhhh-nnnnnnnn…" Chad drawls.

"Duuuuuuuude…" Dan says.

Chad grumbles.

Dan furrows his lips.

Chad flips Dan the bird.

Dan picks up an empty beer bottle and throws it across the room at Chad.

"What the fuck!?" Chad yells, arms flailing in defense.

The room is suddenly charged with wild aggrievement.

A fight breaks out.

It's gross.

Chad and Dan go at each other. A lot of hand slapping. It's gross and I hate it. And contrary to my recent attraction to male battles of domination, does nothing for me, possibly because of the lack of actual muscles and physical faculty of the men involved.

I don't want to get into all the details, but the donnybrook ends semi-amicably, and when the game on TV is over some of the boys actually go out onto the snowy backyard and throw a football around, albeit halfheartedly.

Needless to say, I'm blueballed by the whole sordid masculine exercise. I wander to my sewing room and stare at my loom for what seems like an hour. It's weird, I realize. All that has happened, how I've changed.

Weird... sure. But later that night, things get really weird.

IV

I had been in bed for almost two hours, trying to fall asleep. Sandman would not unload his sandy cum into my bloodshot eyes. I was too keyed up. Too tired to fall asleep. And like how when you're too tired to fall asleep, I was too horny to relieve myself too. I had been stroking my pussy for an hour and couldn't make myself climax. I started to cry. Successively more erotic and demanding fantasies, all the way up to imagining Mr. Gronkowski fucking my ass with warping power on the Fifty Yard Line at Gillette Stadium couldn't even do it for me. Nor would softer and more emotional scenes coax me wet: Gronk on one knee spiking a bouquet of roses, bottle of champagne and diamond ring into my butt on the Fifty Yard Line at Gillette Stadium, had little effect as well.

It was becoming clear that masturbating wasn't cutting it. I needed *actual* human contact. Go figure.

Just as I was coming to this conclusion, Dan came into the room.

He was stumbling around, obviously sloppy and drunk.

I steeled myself for the big blow out, a Superbowl-of-Hand-Ringing-Emotional-Confrontation. Could I punch him? Could I be punched? But then Dan runs a tottering fade route into the bathroom. The guys had watched the 4:30 games and then the Sunday Night Game ("I've Been Waiting All Day for Sunday Night") and bloated their guts with more beer than I cared to imagine.

But Dan in the john gave me time to think.

Was I mad and disappointed at how things had become between us? Yes. But was as I mad and disappointed as I was currently horny and desirous of an orgasm? The answer a resounding No.

Lying on the bed, hidden in the sheets, I decided I needed to save my marriage. If only because I needed hot sex and needed it bad. My crotch was crying out in aching need of a hard-dick pounding. God, I wanted to get fucked so bad. So hard so bad.

Dan stumbled out of the bathroom and fell on the bed next to me. Immediately, I jumped up out of the covers, wild with passion.

I know not what I did.

Dan recoiled. "Wh-wh-what the hell?" he stuttered, confused. I jumped his bones, lavishing kisses all over him.

"I'm horny, Dan!"

"Uh…"

"I need it."

"Need what?"

"I want it."

"It?"

"Dick. Hard dick. Oh, let's fuck, Dan. C'mon, it's been a over a fucking week we've fucked."

Dan groaned. His head was swimming with hops. His head fell back on the pillow, his eyes closed.

"Jeezum, Dan. You don't know what this is? Do you honestly forget what it's like to want to bone your wife?"

Dan laughed. Then he slurred: "Listen, woman. I'm wasted. I gotta sleep. Sleeeeep."

I was speechless. God dammit. My panties and bra, the only stitches of fabric covering my female form, crackled with energy and desire to be shredded.

Dan opened an eye and looked up at me. When he saw I was staring at him intently he leaned up on an elbow and eyed me cautiously, like I might do something to him if he fell asleep. Was he afraid of me?

I couldn't take it any longer. I was hot. HOT. Hot with need. And then I blurted it out. Who the hell knows why I said it, but I did…

"Spike me," I said.

"What?"

"Spike me."

"What?"

"Spike me, Daniel, through the goalposts of life."

"What?"

"Like Gronk does."

"What?"

"Do to me what Gronk does to a football."

"What?"

"Here on the bed."

"I'm going to say it again. What?"

"Fuck, I'm turned on," I drawled and began to undo his pants. "C'mon! Fuck me like Gronk!"

Dan froze. His confusion in that micro-moment instantly annoyed me. I want what I want. I'm a curvy gal. I'm full. I know I could take a pounding if I wanted. Take all the force of a forceful forcing… and then beg for more.

"What the hell!" he shouts and recoils, his voice a horrified high pitch.

I am undaunted by his stupidity and lack of *esprit de corps*. His groin is a short distance from me. I go for it again, lunging at his manhood. Dan jumps out of the way even though he's drunk as shit and he falls off the side of the bed.

He butt fumbles back against the wall and I land on the ground in front of him. It's hot action and I'm all fired up now. Something in me jars loose. I'm ready to come. I don't even bother with Dan now—down low, too slow.

I have my own fire.

On my butt I yank my panties off my ass and down my legs. Leaning up a bit, with my back against the bed I squeeze my titties and spread my legs, then proceed to masturbate right in front of my husband.

"Wha th'hell is all dis, Leigh? Wha tha fa?"

"Oh! Oh Gronk," I moan.

"Wha tha fa is dis shi', Leigh?

"You like what you see, big boy?"

"I—"

"Oh yeah, watch me. Watch me play with myself. Fumbleroooohski…"

The physical confrontation with Dan seemed to be the last hurdle in my stymied sex drive. Pleasure surged in me like a rogue wave.

"Look at me, ungh, splitting my own seam, oohh… going deep. You like how I work my slot receiver, like a tight end. Like Gronkowski… Ooh…" I stroked my wet pussy up and down. The whole lower part of my body throbbed, it ached with want.

"Gronkowski?" Dan said. "Tha scumbag monster!? That Patriot!? Wha tha hell!? Why you doing this to me!?"

"Oooh…" I moan in response. I look at Dan, then close my eyes. "Spike me, Dan. Gronk me, yeah. Gronk me, Dan. Gronk me Gronk. Dan-gronk… Ungh…"

Dan got to his feet, wobbled in place. He looked down at me with morbid disgust. As if to kill me with his eyes. He shook his head.

"I'm outta here, you fuckin' perverrrd!" he screamed.

"No… wait," I said in a sultry voice. "Where are you going, spike your dick into me so hard. I want to feel it—spike—oooh…"

"I'mn goin' where-the-fuck ever, bitsh. Fuck you 'n your Gronk talk— McBeery's for a fuggin' drink."

"Yeah fug me Gronnnnnnnk…"

Dan fled the room and I continued fingering myself between the bed and the wall on the floor.

I closed my eyes and within seconds I was caming like a ferocious sex monster. I screamed and shook. The orgasm was a multi-armed mythical firebeast that fisted me everywhere in my jiggly-jellied-body-turned-to-pudding-pounded-by-a-squad-of-offensive-linemen-who'd-offended-my-little-female-form. It was everything I hoped it would be.

But as I evaporated back to reality I heard Dan's car out in the driveway. He was revving the engine.

The engine screamed. It was incredibly loud. Dan floored the gas; the car must have been in park, the drunk idiot. If he actually gets it in drive he might kill someone, I think to myself.

I got up and ran to the front of the house. Suddenly there was a screeching of tires. I made it to the window just in time to see Dan flying out of the driveway in reverse at a 100 mph. I watch in horror as the car rockets across the street and into our neighbor's driveway where it smashes into their car.

The sound of shattering glass and crunching metal echoes throughout the entire neighborhood, like the death rattle of some giant mechanical robot on an empty waste of tundra.

V

The next few weeks are bad, some of the most tense of my life. Dan moves out for a while. Moves in with Chad, ironically enough, then with Craig or Greg, then with another Greg or Craig, crashing on couches like an itinerant practice squad player.

I go numb. What happened to us? I know I had a huge part in driving Dan away that night with my fantastic display, but the truth is that we had drifted apart a long time ago. It was just a dramatic final scene in a long line of more boring ones. Were we compatible any more? I had to admit that I spent less and less time with him and more with my knitting. Was I hiding from life? The whole Gronk thing, silly as it was—I knew it was a sign. I had starting looking for something outside of our relationship, even only on a fantasy level. And that was bad. Our relationship had been bad for so long, I didn't see it. And this whole stupid football masturbation episode was a symptom of the decay of our relationship.

The police get involved with what happened with the car. It's scary. I have to give a statement. It's hard for me to look the policemen in the eye as they question me. I wonder briefly if I should come clean: blurt out that it's my wantonness, my perverted wish for Rob Gronkowski to hammer me with his hammer-cock right in my quivering pussy end-zone that drove Daniel away in a drunken stupor. Somehow though, I manage to leave this bit out. Don't ask, don't tell.

Things look tense for a while, like Dan might be arrested, but finally our neighbor chooses not to press charges.

A week or so after that Dan and I are on the phone, trying to talk things through.

"What happened to us, Leigh, huh?" Dan says.

"A lot of things," I say.

"Hmm, that's true. Maybe."

I don't know what to say. I am silent.

"Do you think we can get back to before…?" he trails off.

"Before what? Before my sordid sexual display or before football or before we were even married when we used to have fun and stay up late, partying, licking each other's bodies, making each other laugh, never wanting to be apart?"

"Yeah," he says, kind of enigmatically. "Yeah."

"Your drinking—"

"Is out of control, I know. It's dumb."

"It's not dumb. It's scary. You could be in jail. What if you had made it out to a main road? What if you had hit someone? Or driven into the neighbor's living room? What if—"

"I know, I know, I know…" Dan laments. "I used to hate alcohol. Hate it. Such a waste of time getting wasted. Somewhere along the line it just entered my life and didn't leave. And the football. So easy to just sit and watch and drink. With the booze… It's like I'm numbing myself to life with it."

This strikes a chord with me. "Yeah," I say. "I know what you mean."

Dan takes my positive response a little too positively and quickly though. "So I can come home now? You know, to *my own home?*" he says, a little too peremptorily.

Has he been playing me? I feel like I've been played. Perhaps I've been played my whole life.

"You want to come back?" I say.

"Yeah, Jesus, Leigh, of course. I'm so sorry for what I've done. For all the crap I've put you through." Again, this seems like the exact right thing to say. I'm not sure I believe it.

"I'll take you back on only one condition," I say.

"Okay, what?" he says.

I smiled into the phone.

"Shoot," he says. "I'll do anything."

"You have to take me to a Patriots game."

VI

I don't know if you've ever been to a professional sports game, but the general effect is one of besotting unpleasantness.

The stadium atmosphere that day was stupefying. There were so many people everywhere screaming. It was unnerving. I was used to a quiet room, the steady pulse of a loom or knitting needles the only sound to bristle the silence—maybe a radio tuned to a classical station when I was feeling raucous.

Never had I felt such raucousness, as if the number of people losing their heads would cause the earth to fly off its orbit and fall into the sun...

After much wrangling over the phone, and backtracking to a place of disaccord in our relationship, Dan finally relented. "Fine!" he'd shouted. "God dammit, fine!" A week later we were on our way east across the good state of Connecticut to a Patriot's home game in Foxboro. We had amazing seats too. Tenth row, right behind one of the end zones.

Why had I done it?

Was it to see Gronk in action or just to teach Dan a lesson? These were the questions I asked myself. But as the game got underway, neither of them mattered. I just wanted to get the hell out of there.

We were surrounded by screaming idiots. Suddenly everything I hated about America but perhaps didn't believe actually existed except as a foil for me on the internet was thrown in my face.

The game got underway and it was really hard to follow what was going on without the commentators explaining things and all the zoom-ins and stuff. And plus the closest Gronk ever got to me was about a hundred feet—talk about blueball city. I'd even brought a big old blanket with me just in case I needed some "private time."

Worst of all though… *The women.*

There were women all around us. Football

women. Screaming just as loud as the men, waving signs and wearing authorized team gear. It was evident they didn't understand a lick about what was going on on the field—just that things were happening and a certain pageantry was involved and frothing fervor was required. The fervor they displayed in cheering for the teams could easily be misconstrued as panic and fear of being outed for not understanding anything that was happening around them.

"Jesus, this is terrible!" I shouted to Dan.

Dan had been in a funk all game. Looking morose. Only drinking two beers per quarter rather than his usual four.

"I know—the fucking Patriots. I can't believe we're here either," he said.

"No, not just the Patriots. The whole thing. The game. Football. The world. Us."

"What do you mean?"

"I thought coming here, seeing Gronk, seeing how football worked in real life, might create a spark for us. But I don't see it happening. You're being a curmudgeon. Why the hell do you watch football but hate football so much at the same time? We're here right now, watching the very thing you spend so much time watching. I don't know who you are any more, Dan. You used to want to do things and not be content to watch. You painted. You had that cartoon in the paper. You played the piano. We did karaoke. We went to the Olive Garden and *destroyed* the free bread sticks. We had dreams. What happened to all that?"

Dan had been listening to me with growing complexity of emotion. He tried to answer, only stuttered. We met eyes. We stared into the worlds of each other's eyes for what seemed like an eternity. Was he crying?

"Leigh, I don't—"

But before he could speak the crowd around us surged, the volume increased a thousand-fold. People stood. We stayed sitting, looking into each other's eyes, knowing that our marriage was coming to an end. Sort of as a side note, I watched Dan as he turned to look, perhaps involuntarily, out at the field to see what was happening. If there was any proof that we were done, it was this: We were breaking up and he could have said anything—ANYTHING—to get me to stick with him, but instead he chose to be distracted by a football game. A silly, stupid, meaningless game that for some reason the general populace had deemed important enough to inflate to disproportionate favor.

"Dan…"

He didn't respond.

"I want to go home."

He turned his whole body to the field.

"Now. Dan. I want to go home now!" I shouted.

After all that, finally he spoke. "Come on!" he shouted.

"Finally!" I shouted.

But instead of going out the row and up the aisle he grabbed my hand, yanked me up out of my seat, and pulled me in the direction of the field, down towards the edge.

"What the hell are you doing?"

"Look!" he shouted.

I follow his outstretched arm.

I see it.

Out on the field a chaotic assortment of colors collects itself into a recognizable pattern…

The ball is in the air. I follow it with my eyes, a beautiful arc—a long ball. The crowd collectively gasps. They see who it's for.

Yes: Gronk.

Gronk splits the seam, nabs the pigskin. His

two giant mitts snatch the ball from the air. He tucks the thing under his arm and turns upfield. One of the two of his constant companions double-teaming him goes high and is pounded out of the air onto the turf. The low guy fares no better. He dives at Gronk's feet but has about as much luck under him as a frog would under a tractor trailer barreling down I-95.

Dan and I are at the end of the aisle now, he's dragged me down along the first row just off the right of center of the end zone. The end zone, in fact, that Gronkowski is now running toward.

"What the hell are you doing?"

"I could ask you the same question."

"What do you mean?"

"Well, you brought me here. You know I didn't want to come, but I came because I love you."

"Really?"

"Yes, of course, Leigh. I always have," Dan says, squeezes my hand and looks me deep in the eyes. "I've just been so *lost* lately. I don't know. I don't know if it's actually just because I'm a Jets fan or my head's all muzzy from watching so much football on TV."

Dan has to shout all this. The crowd around

us is going bananas.

"I don't know what to say, I mean…" I yell at him, my heart melting.

"And to show you how serious about how much I love you, I'm going to give you Gronk."

"Huh?"

"Pain heals, chicks dig scars and glory lasts forever!"

"Wait! What?"

Before I know what the hell is going on, Dan yanks me hard by the hand again and we go flying over the wall onto the field below.

How the stadium staff and the various police officers on the field don't see us right away I have no idea. But I do have some idea, *mais oui*, now that I've watched replays of the incident hundreds of times, over and over again, on the TV and in my mind, since the most romantic and selfless gesture the world has ever seen happened.

The staff and the cops don't see us because they're distracted. Dan timed it perfectly. They're all turned on their heels to watch Gronk.

Out on the field Gronk steamrolls the free safety, the last defender standing between him and the end zone. The roar of the crowd coincides with us hitting the turf. Gronk strolls into the end zone by himself, a victorious gladiator in the middle of the Coliseum. There isn't a teammate or an opponent within thirty yards of him. But there *is* a couple of rejuvenated perverts.

"What the hell are you doing you madman!" I scream.

Gronk spins around with the football in the middle of the end zone. He's like a tornado. A gigantic whirling dervish. The arm comes up. The ball is hoisted like a human sacrifice. Here comes the spike.

Dan has me by the hand. I'm like a ragdoll in his grip. It's a strength I've never experience from him before.

We're on the field now. All that space. The space of the stadium is too much to take in, out there in front of all those eyes. I am dizzy. Vertigo makes my legs weak.

Which must have helped Dan in his mission, because just as Gronk launches the ball downward, we cross into the end zone, just to the right of Gronk, and Dan whips me down beneath him.

Really, the timing was perfect.

The ball comes down with unholy speed, and my body goes careening underneath Gronk, my limbs flailing. I do a somersault, ass over teakettle, my legs are spread open. Just as the ball comes flying out of Gronk's hand, and in my wild rotating movement, I am on all-fours, my legs spread open shoulder-width apart as if I'm about to take it doggy-style.

Which I do.

In front of the entire country, Gronk's spike impacts right between my butt-cheeks.

I don't know how to explain exactly to you what happened to me since it was so otherworldly. There really is no accounting for it. But I can tell you that it felt *amazing*.

Gronkowski's ball unleashes a rainbow of sensation throughout my body. Pleasure shoots magically in every direction like an explosion of sparks. It jettisons jiggling ribbons of joy to every part of my body. It feels as though I am being fucked by a stampeding horde of marauders. It is shocking in its speed and power how instantaneously I am transformed from a tumbling ragdoll into an orgasmic nuclear explosion. Like in Star Wars when that guy shoots the one tiny little spot on the space ship to blow it up—that's exactly what happens to me. Somehow, the pointy edge of the ball has found my secret spot, the magic invisible place where I am the most a woman.

The ball goes flying elsewhere. I continue my spinning motion. I fly end-over-end and I land on my back, facing upward into the sky. It is here that I climax. The sky, the stadium, all of Mother Nature looks down upon me. I shake uncontrollably as if I'm having a fit.

I mean, really. I am.

Gronk has his touchdown, and lying on the end zone like a princess on a luxurious bed one hundred and sixty feet wide and thirty feet deep, I have my royal orgasm.

I am wet, my pants are soaked, and my pussy is throbbing. My whole body throbs in time with the strongest orgasm I ever had in my entire life. I laugh. I cry. Love envelops me. I look up into Gronk's confused eyes. I laugh again. He had no idea what was about to happen to him. And then I cry again because… well, who the hell knows why. Because of the rotation of the planet, because of love and all of humanity bundled together on this silly planet.

A thick, rich, bootylicious sweat encapsulates my physique. You never go broke making a profit and you never die of bonershrivelry if you get the pussy juicy in the juicing place, I think to myself.

"Oh… wow!" I moan up into Gronk's eyes.

He is smiling. "Wow is right," Gronk says. We both laugh.

VII

Relatively rapidly, stadium security cottons on to what they have let through in their negligence. They capture me and then Dan.

We both go willingly.

Hands quivering with insulted authority upon us, we are marched into a dark chute under the stands.

"Oh… oh… God… Thank you Dan, thank you…" I moan. I think I'm still climaxing. In the clutches of the police I am still having multiple orgasms. They have to carry me as if I'm some kind of a protestor. My legs are Jello.

"Anything for you, Leigh."

"I love you," I moan, my voice echoing long and warbled down the tunnel.

"I love you too," Dan says.

We're deposited in a holding cell. Charges are pressed against us. And our lives change pretty heavily afterward. We become overnight sensations on the internet. Animated GIFs are made of us, Dan and I. Memes refract in a million directions. "Bagronkadonk Chick" is my favorite eponym of myself, coined by a twitter user named @laceynoonan. I RT it to my 2.3 million followers. My etsy store, chock full of my handsome knittings and crochets, takes off like a rocket…

* * *

Everyone has their favorite Gronk moment. His big plays. His stratospheric leaps of athleticism. I have two: The first time I saw a Gronk and the last time. The first one of course was pretty great. It caused me to open up sexually and to come to terms fully with life and how I was running away from it. That moment was pretty special to me, but the second is really the best…

The Gronking out on the field at Foxboro was the one that reminded Dan and I how much we loved each other.

It was truly a Gronking to remember.

ABOUT THE AUTHOR

Well, let me tell you about good ol' Lacey Noonan. Lacey lives on the east coast with her kinks, perversions and obsessions. And possibly a husband or two.

When not sailing, sampling fine whiskeys or making veggie tacos, you can find her reading and writing steamy, strange, silly, psychological and sexy stories.

And when she gets down on her knees during the day for the man, she is a web designer and developer.

Twitter
https://twitter.com/laceynoonan

Email
laceynoonan123@gmail.com

Made in the USA
Middletown, DE
05 January 2015